Blue Suede Killer

Suede

Killer

Book Sixteen in

The INNcredibly Sweet Series

By

Summer Prescott

Author's note: I'd love to hear your thoughts on my books, the storylines, and anything else that you'd like to comment on—reader feedback is very important to me. My contact information, along with some other helpful links, is listed below. If you'd like to be on my list of "folks to contact" with updates, release and sales notifications, etc.... just shoot me an email and let me know. Thanks for reading!

Also…

… if you're looking for more great reads, I am proud to announce that Summer Prescott Books publishes several popular series by Cozy author Patti Benning, as well as Carolyn Q. Hunter, Blair Merrin, Susie Gayle and more! Check out my book catalog http://summerprescottbooks.com/book-catalog/ for their delicious stories.

Contact Info for Summer Prescott:

Twitter: @summerprescott1

Blog and Book Catalog:

http://summerprescottbooks.com

Email: summer.prescott.cozies@gmail.com

Please note: If you receive any correspondence from addresses other than those listed here, it is not from me, even if it claims to be.

And... look me up on Facebook—let's be friends!

Foreword from Summer Prescott:

To say that 2016 was a challenging year is quite the understatement. I lost my precious mother the day after Thanksgiving, and seeing her battle cancer broke my heart, but she never gave up. She was strong, determined and full of personality right up to the end, her courage and sweetness were a constant inspiration. I could be strong because she was strong, I could love unconditionally because she loved unconditionally.

It was so difficult to write during the final months of 2016, as I suffered through grief and loss, (I even forgot to write Book 12 in the INNcredibly Sweet series and went right on to Book 13), but write I did, because she wanted me to go on. When I said goodbye to her for the last time, she said two things to me – the first of course, was, "I love you," and as I dissolved into tears, despite my vow to try to stay strong and positive, the last thing my beloved mother ever said to me was, "It's going to be okay." Yes, even in the midst of her tremendous pain, even in the certain face of death, her impulse was to reassure me, to give me comfort. This is who she was, and this is why so many loved her.

So I struggled and mourned, and continue to miss her every day, but I've carried on, because she wanted me to, and because I could honor her by doing so. Everything that I see and everything that I do is dramatically changed because of the fact that I'll never hear that sweet voice on the phone again, and will never be embraced in her warm hug. I appreciate life and the little things, and have been trying to treat others the way that she always did, making everyone that she knew feel special and loved. I'm an introvert, so part of the way that I show appreciation is through my writing. I put characteristics of awesome people that I meet into my characters, and try to show the good things in humanity – love, trust, relationships – even in the midst of a new murder every couple of weeks.

Dear Readers, thank you for your patience with me when I went weeks between releases, and thank you for reading and enjoying the books and characters that I love so much. Your support has helped me make it through. Now, as soon as I get my new puppy, Elvis, busy chewing on his toy rather than my shoe, I'll finish writing another book! Enjoy!

TABLE OF CONTENTS

BLUE SUEDE KILLER

Book Sixteen in The INNcredibly Sweet Series

.

CHAPTER ONE

P etite, blonde Melissa Gladstone-Beckett tapped her foot impatiently. She stared out the front window of her shop, Cupcakes in Paradise, as if she could conjure her husband into appearing through sheer force of will. She and her handsome, clever mate, Detective Chas Beckett, who would soon be leaving the Calgon, Florida police force now that he'd opened up his own private investigations firm, were going house hunting.

Since they'd moved to the sleepy beachside community of Calgon, they'd owned, operated and lived in the Beach House B&B, which was located on a lovely sugar-sand beach. It had only been recently, when Chas had decided to open his own firm, that the couple had decided to sell the inn, but Missy would still keep the cupcake shop which was right across the parking lot from it. Baking was her refuge, and she loved the joy that she brought to her customers when they sampled her luscious cupcakes. There was no way in the world that she'd give up her cozy little shop, which was decorated in Florida pastels.

Their realtor, whom she hadn't yet met in person yet, was due to arrive at any moment, after which they'd embark upon their house hunting adventure, and Missy's stomach did little flip-flops of anticipation.

"Oh, thank goodness," she breathed when she saw Chas's car pull up.

Her husband and his lead investigator, Spencer Bengal, arrived right on time, as usual. Spencer was a young Marine veteran who had been specially trained by Chas's ultra-wealthy family to be a bodyguard for the Beckett heir, which Chas and Missy had only discovered recently. He'd been working at the behest of Chas's late father for years, and had become like family to Missy and Chas, long before they discovered his true purpose in their lives. He'd been living in the basement of the inn, and acting as caretaker, but now that Missy and Chas were changing direction, Spencer would need to find a new living situation as well.

The Marine was going to take care of business at the cupcake shop while Missy and Chas went house hunting. He and Chas were going through some of the Calgon police department's cold cases to keep busy, since the PI firm had just opened, but as yet, no new cases had come in, so he was available to help out. Missy loved leaving the young man in charge periodically. Spencer was a bit of a neat freak and a perfectionist, so every time she returned after leaving the shop in his care, all surfaces were sparkling, everything was neatly arranged and put away, and her ingredients were alphabetized.

Hugging the striking young man, who had tied back his black wavy hair for the occasion, Missy grinned up at him.

"Are you ready to do some frosting?" she asked.

"Your wish is my command," Spencer flashed the dimples which, unbeknownst to him, devastated the hearts of females, young and old alike. "What's the plan for today?"

"I have twelve dozen Blue Suede Cupcakes for you to frost while you're here, and I want them to look really special," Missy handed him a large baggie which contained little black guitars.

"Wait...what in the world is a Blue Suede Cupcake?" The young man raised his eyebrows.

"It's the most decadent vanilla cupcake you've ever tasted, filled with vanilla pudding, frosted with vanilla buttercream and topped with a little sugar-sculpted guitar."

"So what makes them blue? And why are you making blue cupcakes anyway?"

"What makes them blue is my little secret, and they're for the Elvis impersonators convention that they're having downtown this weekend."

"That's awesome," the young man grinned. "I love Elvis."

"Oh, me too, honey. Me, too. When I found out that the convention was coming to Calgon, I had to fan myself," Missy's Louisiana accent got just a tad thicker as she waved her hand in front of her face, making the Marine crack up.

"What about you, Chas? Are you a fan?" he asked.

"I enjoy the music, yes. I'm just not quite as vehement about my appreciation as my lovely wife is," the detective kissed the top of his wife's head, slipping his arm around her.

"Oh, you're just jealous because I said Elvis was the first man I ever wanted to marry," she teased, poking him playfully.

"Oh?" Spencer couldn't hide his amusement.

"Yes, indeed. I was six years old when I told my mama that I was going to marry Elvis. Broke my heart when she said he already had a wife."

"Clearly you were meant for someone else," Spencer looked pointedly at Chas.

"Yes, I was, and he sings to me, too," Missy beamed up at her husband.

"Does he now?" The Marine was enjoying the whole exchange just a bit too much, but Chas was spared having to answer by the arrival of Lizbeth Walker, realtor extraordinaire.

"You must be Missy!" The perfectly manicured, impeccably frosted woman smiled, extending a hand heavy with gems.

"Hi Lizbeth, it's so nice to meet you finally. This is my husband, Chas."

"Well, you lucky girl. Nice to meet you, Chas. I've heard some wonderful things about you," the realtor shook his hand, giving him a swift once-over. "And just who might this be?" Lizbeth focused on Spencer with obvious interest.

"Spencer Bengal," the young man smiled professionally and shook her hand.

"Well, hello, tiger," she purred, then gave a throaty laugh. "Will we have the pleasure of your company today?"

"No. I'm just here to mind the store," he shrugged.

"This man, in a store full of cupcakes? Someone pinch me, I've got to be dreaming," she teased, making the Marine blush a bit.

"We're so eager to see some houses today," Missy rescued him, and he took the opportunity to duck into the kitchen.

"Well, my lovely southern belle, I have some darling homes to show you two. Shall we?" she gestured toward the door.

"We shall," Chas replied, walking beside his wife, his hand in the small of her back.

When the trio got to the door, Lizbeth turned around.

"Take care, Tiger!" she called, opening the door.

Spencer, banging pans around in the kitchen, pretended not to hear.

CHAPTER TWO

L izbeth Walker's massive hybrid SUV was the color of pearls, inside and out, which seemed an entirely appropriate choice for the polished professional. Missy and Chas climbed into the plush interior, which smelled faintly of expensive perfume, and looked through the listing sheets that she handed them.

"They all look very nice," Missy remarked, flipping through the sheets.

"There are some wonderful options in there," Lizbeth nodded. "We'll start off with the one on Franklin Drive and go from there."

To say that the house on 914 Franklin Drive was grand would be a tremendous understatement. Lizbeth pulled into the circular drive in front of pillars that looked like they belonged in a Roman palace, behind which stood a pair of substantial and intimidating mahogany doors.

"Wow," Missy whispered, her eyes wide.

"Oh honey, wait till you see the inside," Lizbeth gave her a knowing smile.

Behind the imposing doors lay a room too large to be called just a foyer, which was floored in pink and white marble. The artwork on the walls and antique furnishings took Missy's breath away.

"My favorite color is pink," she commented, feeling much like a fish out of water.

"Interesting flooring choice," Chas remarked.

"Let's take a tour," Lizbeth led them further into the massive home.

There were four bedrooms besides the master suite, each with its own bath, formal and casual living and dining areas, a chef's kitchen, a workout suite, and an indoor/outdoor pool. The extensive grounds were manicured, so much so that Missy felt guilty about stepping on the grass, and featured fountains, stone benches and a huge outdoor kitchen and entertaining area. After looking through every room, and exploring the grounds, the trio stood back in the pink foyer.

"So, what do you think? Isn't it fabulous?" Lizbeth spread her hands, gesturing to the room around them.

Chas, who grew up on an estate which made this home seem like a shanty, merely nodded.

"Maybe too fabulous," Missy offered in a small voice.

"What do you mean, honey? These pink floors just scream Missy Beckett, don't they?" The realtor raised her eyebrows.

"I do like the floors. There are several things that I like. The pool is stunning, but…"

"But…?" Lizbeth prompted.

"It doesn't feel homey," Missy shrugged, a bit embarrassed. "I feel like I'd be living in a museum. I don't think the girls would be comfortable here."

"The girls?"

"My dogs. Toffee is a golden retriever and Bitsy is a maltipoo."

"Oh, you have one of those little purse doggies, how cute! Did you dye her ears pink or anything?"

"Uh…no. They're both pretty active, outdoorsy girls," Missy smiled fondly, thinking of her furry babies.

"Oh," Lizbeth blinked at her for a moment. "Does that mean that you need a separate yard for the dogs?"

"Oh no, they live in the house, we just like to go for walks and play in the park or on the beach."

"Okay then, there are a couple of beachfront homes on the list that might be just what you're looking for," she smiled. "Shall we press on?"

"Yes, let's," Missy agreed, letting out a subtle sigh of relief.

**

After a day of trudging through homes that reminded Missy of an episode of Lifestyles of the Rich and Shameless, they headed back toward home, the interior of the car very quiet. Missy felt guilty that Lizbeth had worked so hard and she hadn't liked any of the selections, but hoped that after spending so much time together, the realtor might have a better idea now of what they were looking for. She stared out the window feeling tired and defeated, watching the palm trees and flowers passing by.

"Hey," Missy sat up straight in her seat suddenly. "What's that?" she pointed to a sign on the left.

"Oh honey, you wouldn't be interested in that property," Lizbeth chuckled.

The sign was in front of a lane that was a bit overgrown, and as they passed by, Missy caught a glimpse of a large house, way down the lane.

"Why not? Can we see it?" she asked, excited for the first time today.

"It's been abandoned for months, and it's not in very good shape," Lizbeth made a face.

Chas, seeing the sudden light in his beloved's eyes, broke in. "If it's vacant, let's stop by and take a look. That is, if you have time."

"I cleared my entire day for you two. If you want to see this one, I'll show it to you, but I can already tell you, you'll be disappointed," she warned.

"Yes, we definitely want to see it," Missy nodded happily.

Lizbeth turned the SUV around, and as the huge vehicle entered the lane, tree branches brushed over its top. The lane was unpaved and there were ruts in the gravel which bounced them around so much that Missy had to grab the armrest.

"You're sure about this?" Lizbeth asked, her voice tight as the neglected house came into view.

Missy's eyes were shining. "Positive," she murmured.

CHAPTER THREE

C arla Mayhew was an Interior Designer who had purchased the inn from Missy and Chas when they mentioned the possibility that they might want to sell. The widow had been Missy's first friend when the couple had moved to Calgon from Louisiana, and was thrilled at the prospect of operating the inn. She had helped Missy redecorate it in the very beginning and planned to make a few more changes once she closed on the property.

Carla was shadowing Maggie, the lithe, silver-haired innkeeper that the Becketts had "inherited" with the inn, to try and learn the ropes before she took over as owner, and was in a tizzy trying to help prepare for the arriving Elvises that would be staying at the Inn. Every room was booked for the convention, and every room had at least one Elvis impersonator staying in it. Carla thought that the phenomenon was strange, and was glad only for the extra business, while Missy was ecstatic, loving the sounds of the guys practicing their songs.

There were Elvises of all shapes, sizes and ages. Some wore wigs as part of their costumes, others dyed their own hair black and styled it in the iconic pompadour, and some even wore blue contact lenses to look like a more convincing version of the King. The costumes were flamboyant and wonderful, hanging in closets, on shower rods and over the tops of doors, or, in a few cases, laid out reverently on beds or chairs. To Missy it was an entertaining and colorful circus of music, outfits and outgoing strangers.

"This is the weirdest hobby I've ever seen," Carla said as she shook her head, having plopped down in a chair at Cupcakes in Paradise for a much-needed break.

"Ha! Clearly you've never been to Louisiana. I think it's adorable," Missy grinned. "And I love the music. All my favorite songs are playing at the inn all day long."

"I know, I've been taking ibuprofen," Carla rubbed her temples.

"Not a fan?"

"Maybe I would be, if I didn't have to worry about linens and shampoos and how many different seatings I need to host for breakfast," she sighed.

"Maggie is there, and that woman is always on top of her game," Missy reassured her stressed out friend. "Don't worry, you two will get through this just fine. Want a Blue Suede Cupcake? I'm boxing them up now," she offered, knowing that cupcakes were often the solution to life's minor challenges.

"No, I'm not eating carbs these days."

"No wonder you're stressed," Missy chuckled. "Are you drinking caffeine these days?"

"Goodness yes, it's how I survive."

"One large coffee coming right up."

"You're an angel," Carla accepted the steaming mug gratefully.

"An *Angel in Disguise*?" Missy teased her friend with the title of an Elvis song.

"Very funny," the designer stuck out her tongue.

Missy giggled, busily loading Spencer's perfectly frosted cupcakes into boxes to take to the convention. "Oh, hey. I may need a ton of help from you soon."

"She says to the woman who is currently worn to a frazzle and re-evaluating her life choices," Carla commented dryly.

"No, this would be fun, you'd love it," she promised.

"Do tell," the designer drawled.

"Yes, do tell," Echo Willis chimed in, coming in the kitchen door.

Echo and Missy were best friends who met nearly every morning to start their day with cupcakes and coffee. The two had met and formed a strong bond in Louisiana, and just before Missy moved to Florida with Chas, Echo had gone back to her home state, California. The friends couldn't stand being so far away from each other, and the free-spirited, red-haired vegan soon followed Missy's lead and moved to Calgon. They'd been inseparable ever since. Carla and Echo had not gotten along at all when Echo first came to town, but they'd grown to accept each other…for the most part.

"Hey, darlin'! I didn't hear you come in," Missy gave the new wife and mother a kiss on the cheek.

"I slipped in the back, hoping I'd score some fresh coffee," she held up her mug and sat down next to Carla. "Morning, sunshine," she grinned, her voice tinged with sarcasm.

"Do you know how many times I've heard "hey, mama" in the last few days?" Carla complained.

"Who could ever tire of hearing that?" Echo ribbed her, chuckling. "So, what did I interrupt?"

"I was just about to share some potentially interesting news," Missy's eyes lit up.

"Well, spit it out woman!" Echo ordered, helping herself to a vegan cupcake from the platter that Missy had set out. She'd begun using cupcake papers that were marked with V so there'd be no trouble telling which cupcakes were which.

"Chas and I may have found a house."

"Oh, that's awesome!" Echo exclaimed, while Carla sat up and became interested, her coffee kicking in.

"Well, it could be," Missy bit her lip for a moment. "I think Lizbeth thinks I'm crazy."

"Lizbeth thinks that she is the sun around which the rest of us revolve," Carla commented.

"You know her?" Echo asked.

"I've done work for some of her clients and have run into her socially, yes."

"She's very nice," Missy hastened to explain. "But I think that she thinks just because Chas has an unlimited budget that we want something ostentatious, and I'm just not comfortable with that," she confessed.

"So tell us about the potential new house," Echo prompted.

"Well, it needs a little work…"

"That's not a problem, is it?" was Echo's encouraging reply.

"Wait," Carla raised an eyebrow. "How much work? Where is this place?"

"It's on its own lane, right off of Fairview Heights," Missy began.

"Holy moly, the old Sorenson place?" Carla demanded.

"Yes. You know it?"

"I designed the interior years ago, when they were building it. That place had gold-leafed wall paper, solid gold fixtures, and every high-end finish that I could get my hands on, but it's been deserted for a while. I heard that vandals came in and stripped it. Why on earth would you want that place?"

"I know why," Echo smiled at Missy. "She always loves the underdog. Whether it's a stray pet, a person who is down on their luck, or a cupcake shop that succeeds against all odds, Missy always wants to give things a chance. Even a musty old house."

"I think that's part of it," Missy nodded. "I look at it and I see potential. I think it could be so cute and homey. It looks awful, inside and out right now, but I think Chas and I could make it our own."

"Well, you'd certainly have your work cut out for you," Carla shook her head.

"Or you," Echo nudged the designer playfully.

"Well, I do love a challenge," she sighed. "And if it will get me away from the Elvis group for a while…"

"Hey, yeah! Can the three of us go see it tonight?" Echo asked.

"I'd love to show it to you! Let me give Lizbeth a call. Carla, are you in?" Missy reached for her phone.

"As long as Maggie can spare me," she shrugged.

"Oh, I have a feeling Maggie will be just fine," Missy smiled and dialed the realtor's number.

CHAPTER FOUR

J ack Swartham checked his look in the mirror and smoothed down his glossy black sideburns with his hands.

"Looking good, baby!" His wife, Lotta cooed, checking him out in the mirror.

"Well, thank you, mama," he replied in his best Elvis voice, curling his lip just a bit. He'd worked hard on getting the lip curl just right, so that it was a sexy pout rather than a sneer. It had won him many a competition in the past.

Jack was a pro in the Elvis scene. He made his living performing and competing as the King, and his reflection in the mirror told him that he only had maybe a decade left in his profession. He was just now starting to show signs of wear and tear from being on the road most of the time. There were thin lines at the corner of his eyes, and creases in his forehead, but he still looked good, and would perform as long as he could.

Lotta was a dental receptionist who rarely traveled with him, but when he'd said he was going to sunny Florida, after a long winter in their Champaign, Illinois home, she'd insisted upon going with him.

"Are you going to take me out tonight, since you'll be busy the rest of the weekend?" She batted her eyes at him.

Lotta wasn't afraid to be seen in public with a man who quite obviously made his living pretending to be a dead rock star; she loved it. She loved the stares and attention, and loved being on the arm of her very own version of the sexiest man who'd ever lived. She wore her hair and makeup like Elvis's wife Priscilla had, back in the sixties, and dressed like a proper groupie would. They made quite the striking couple, and she reveled in the attention, particularly when folks stopped them, asking to take their picture.

"I can't tonight, baby doll," Jack popped the collar on the outfit that he was trying on.

He'd brought an entire wardrobe with him, and would decide which ones that he'd wear to the convention after meeting with some of the other Elvises to make sure that he didn't duplicate anyone else's costume. Lotta was particularly enamored of his G.I. Blues look, but he'd grown his sideburns out, so now he was pretty much locked into a more mod Elvis look, which appealed to her in a different way.

"Why?" she said, wincing at how whiny her voice had sounded.

"I gotta go over to the Hilton, downtown, and practice my duet with Britney. We're one of the first acts in the lineup on opening night, so it's gotta be solid, little lady," he chucked her under the chin, then went back to assessing his outfit.

"Britney? Again? Why do they always pair you with her?" Now Lotta no longer cared that she sounded whiny. Her contempt for the young Marilyn Monroe impersonator ran deep.

"Because we're both top contenders, baby. I tell you that every time. You gotta stop makin' a fuss every time I have a gig with Britney," he gave her a look.

"Funny how she always seems to end up at the same conventions that you do," Lotta's eyes narrowed.

"Yeah, hysterical. It's not like there are only a few places that an impersonator can go to make a living or anything," he mocked her, his patience wearing thin. He didn't need this kind of distraction the night before a competition.

"How come you never sing with me? Elvis and Priscilla? That would be so cute," she pouted.

"Cuz you can't carry a tune in a bucket, honey bun. I'm going to go practice with Britney tonight, and you can go buy something pretty to wear for my celebration dinner when I win this thing," Jack reached into his pocket, pulled out a hundred dollar bill and tucked it into her cleavage.

"Fine, but you get home early, and make sure it's nothing but singing going on," she warned.

"There never is, doll," he smirked and opened the case containing his blue contact lenses.

**

"That Jack Swartham better keep his hands to himself. I don't know why they paired you with that amateur anyhow. Shoulda been me. My hair is way more authentic. He doesn't even have his hair shaved into the right hairline shape," Britney Lancer's husband, Rocko, muttered, lighting up a cigarette.

"Rocko, you can't smoke that in here, we'll get fined, put that out," the buxom bleach-blonde ordered, smoothing on a smear of red lipstick. "You know you ain't got nothin' to worry about. I only got eyes for you, pookie-pie," she gave him a sultry Marilyn look that she'd been perfecting.

"Yeah, it ain't *your* eyes I'm worried about," he growled, stealing up on her from behind and nibbling her neck.

"Stop it," she giggled. "I just got done with my hair, you'll ruin it," she pushed him away.

"Gotta look good for Jack?" Rocko grimaced.

"No, it's a public rehearsal, dumb-dumb. What if there are casino people there? Or Hollywood people? Geez, Rock, do you ever think about anything but your own stupid Elvis competitions?" she challenged, hands on hips.

"Is Jack my competition?" he shot back.

"Only on the stage, you big lug," she sighed. "I gotta go. You better be in a good mood when I get back, or you're sleepin' on the couch."

"Go sing. But he better not touch you," Rocko hollered as Britney gave the door a resounding slam.

**

The stage manager at the convention center stood beside the curtain, directing the flow of the show. Jack Swartham and Britney Lancer were on stage, getting ready to start their duet, when Lotta Swartham and Rocko Lancer arrived from two different directions, standing behind him.

"Evening," Rocko gave Lotta a quick nod.

"Hey, Rock," she replied, her eyes glued to the pair on the stage. "Come to watch?"

"Yeah. You?"

"Yeah," she nodded. "You know, it just seems funny, the way the association always pairs those two together. I mean, they're both good, but you'd think they'd want to change things up a bit every once in a while," she mused, noting how the two performers were standing awfully close and laughing.

"They don't," the stage manager said flatly, turning around to look at them.

"Whaddya mean they don't?" Rocko frowned.

"The association doesn't pair anyone. If you want to partner, you have to sign up for it and get it approved," the bearded man shrugged.

Rocko and Lotta exchanged a long look, as realization hit them both.

"Hey Lotta, ya wanna get outta here and grab a drink?"

"You better believe I do," she nodded, a determined look on her face.

The stage manager turned slightly to watch them go, shaking his head.

CHAPTER FIVE

"Wow, this place is creepy. We can't stay long since there's no electricity, right?" Echo wandered around inside the abandoned estate, never losing sight of Missy.

"Right, we won't be able to see much, once the sun starts to go down."

"What a pity," Carla commented dryly, standing in the center of the foyer, arms folded.

"I'm so glad that Lizbeth gave us a key so that we could come out on our own," Missy said, excitement coloring her voice.

"She probably didn't want to get her lily white pantsuit dirty," Carla raised an eyebrow.

"Meow," Echo scolded the designer. "What's your issue with her?"

"Let's just say that we draw from the same pool of eligible bachelors, and Lizbeth likes to muddy the waters," Carla made a face.

"Ouch. I'm so glad I'm not single anymore," Echo raised her eyebrows.

"Betcha never thought you'd say that," Missy teased. "You gals ready to go on a tour?"

"The faster we look at it, the better chance we have of making it out of here alive," Carla muttered.

"I so missed your optimism and pleasant personality," Echo gave her a pointed look.

They wandered through what had once been a spacious and beautiful villa, complete with stuccoed walls and a red tile roof. The stucco now was grimy and spotted with mildew, and some of the clay tiles were broken, but to Missy, the place retained a special grandeur, despite its current condition. The rooms were spacious, with soaring windows, all of which needed to be replaced, and Saltillo tile floors throughout the main living areas. There was a large kidney shaped swimming pool in the back, which was filled with an eerie looking green and black sludge. To the left of the pool was a large cabana, and beyond the pool, the unkempt yard stretched at least the length of a football field.

Echo and Missy moved to the edge of the pool, peering down into the water, while Carla waited, arms crossed, on the patio by the house.

"Smells funny," Missy wrinkled her nose.

"Well, at least you know it holds water," Echo teased, then screamed as a small frog leaped from the murky water on the steps and nearly landed on her foot.

Missy burst into a fit of giggles, holding her midsection as she made her way toward the house, where Echo now stood beside Carla, who was trying not to smile.

"Are we done yet?" she deadpanned, when Missy joined them.

"I am," Echo nodded. "It's getting dark, we should go," her eyes darted toward the fence.

"Okay, but let me just show you the master suite first," Missy's giggles were beginning to taper off.

"Fine, but let's make it quick, I need to get home to feed Jasmine."

"Does Kel have her?"

Phillip "Kel" Kellerman was a world-renowned, but locally based artist, who also happened to be Echo's husband, and he adored the ground that she walked on. His wife and their new baby girl were the lights of his life.

"No, Marsha does, but I have the feeding equipment," she gestured at her top.

"Marsha? I haven't met a Marsha. Is she the new nanny?" Missy asked, surprised.

"Yeah, the first gal didn't work out."

She left it at that and the ladies didn't press for more of an answer, moving inside to see the master suite before the sun went down. They ascended a grand staircase that split the house in two, curving both right and left into lofty halls at the top. Missy turned right and headed for an ornate set of double doors at the end of the hall. She opened the left-hand door and walked inside.

"Isn't this amazing?" she breathed.

"Wow, it actually is," Echo nodded.

"I can make this work," even Carla couldn't be cynical.

The room was like a fairytale tower, with floor to ceiling windows on two sides of the expansive suite, and a raised dais for the bed in the middle. There was a slot in the floor at the foot of the bed, which clearly had once held a pop up television, and behind the platform for the bed was the entrance to a closet the size of a large bedroom, and a master bath which featured a multi-jetted shower and a sunken tub which could easily accommodate at least six people.

"Oh, I could see some quality time with wine and candles in there," Echo remarked.

"I can make this a palace," Carla murmured, glancing about and renovating in her mind.

"I don't need a palace," Missy smiled. "Just a sanctuary for us to come home to at the end of the day."

"Say the word and I'll start the drawings," Carla was fully on board now, and had a definite gleam in her eye.

"I have to talk to Chas, but I'm really thinking that this is the way I want to go," she confessed. "We could make it our own instead of moving into a place that someone else envisioned and decorated."

"I think that's a wonderful plan," Echo agreed. "But can you please make the first order of business securing a lawn and pool guy who will clear out all unnecessary wildlife?" she shuddered.

"I'll make note of that," Missy laughed. "Let's go, it's getting dark.

Missy dropped Echo off at her place then went home to her dogs and Chas.

**

When Missy and Chas were snuggled under the covers, the dogs curled up in their bed in the corner of the bedroom, Missy sighed with contentment and gave her dashing husband a big kiss.

"Mmm…" Chas mumbled sleepily. "What was that for?" he smiled, eyes closed.

"Because I'm happy," she confided, running her fingers through his thick dark hair.

"Good. Me, too," his breathing was slowing.

"I know which house I want," she announced.

"Yeah?"

"Yes, I want the secluded, abandoned villa."

"Okay."

"That's it, just okay?" She pushed his arm a bit to get his attention.

"Yep."

"Well, I was hoping you might be excited about it," she murmured, a bit hurt.

"I am. I knew you'd want it, so I already bought it. Can I go to sleep now?" he mumbled again.

"You…I…oh my gosh, Chas, really? You bought it?" she gasped.

"Mmhmm."

"How did you know that I would want that one?" Missy demanded, delighted.

"Because I know my girl."

"Oh Chas, you're the best! I'm the luckiest woman alive, I swear. Oh my goodness, I have so many ideas for the inside and the outside. I know it'll be a while before it's livable, but I can't wait to get things rolling, and I..." Missy stopped her excited rambling and giggled.

Chas was sound asleep and snoring softly. She brushed the hair back from his brow, kissed his cheek and closed her eyes.

"I love you, you amazing man," she murmured, and drifted off to sleep with a smile on her face.

**

Spencer would be the project manager for the renovation, and would consult with Missy, the contractors and Carla on a regular basis, much to Carla's delight. He'd managed to secure floor plans from the city of Calgon's records department, and had accompanied an inspector when an analysis was done of the property. Most of the systems in the house needed to be revamped, so he'd been meeting with electricians, plumbers, HVAC professionals, structural engineers, and general construction contractors. A team of landscapers was already hard at work clearing the land so that the grounds could be completely redone, and stucco experts were already preparing the exterior for a facelift.

The Marine was discussing the placement of flowers, shrubs and trees with the landscaper, when one of the workers who had been working on the pool cabana came running out of the cabana with a dazed look on his face.

"Hey boss, you're going to want to come take a look at this," he told Spencer, then turned to go back to the cabana.

Spencer and the landscaper followed closely behind and entered the semi-darkness of the cabana. The construction worker shined his flashlight on a hole in the wall that had been opened when he had torn down a patch of mildewed drywall.

"Wow," Spencer's eyebrows shot skyward.

"Holy cow," the landscaper breathed.

"Do you have gloves I can borrow?" Spencer asked the construction worker.

"Yeah man, take mine," he tossed them over.

Spencer snugged the gloves on, and stepped toward the wall. Taking the edge of the remaining drywall in both hands, he pulled hard, ripping the drywall down to reveal the studs beneath.

"Whoa," the construction worker breathed.

"Yeah, looks like you're done in here for the day," Spencer tossed him his gloves back and tapped a message to Chas into his watch.

"I'll take it from here. You can join the team inside the house, and let me know if you run into anything like this in there."

"You got it boss," he nodded.

"What's your name?" Spencer asked.

"Joe."

"Thanks, Joe. This is quite a find."

"Yes, sir," he nodded again, then took off for the main house.

Chas arrived roughly ten minutes later, and made his way carefully through the yard filled with debris from the overhaul that was happening outside. He poked his head inside the cabana and found Spencer waiting for him.

"Whatcha got?" he asked, coming into the room.

"Check it out," the Marine replied, shining his light toward the wall.

The detective rocked back on his heels and whistled through his teeth.

"Well, that's quite a find," his eyebrows shot skyward.

"Yeah," Spencer nodded. "We need to get it out of here, and find out where it came from."

"I'll let you take charge of that. You know what to do. If you see Missy, invent whatever reason you can think of and send her home.

I don't want her to set foot on this property until I know how this got here and why."

"I'm with you on that one."

"Need anything?"

"A really big bag," the Marine blew out a breath.

"I have one in my trunk."

.

CHAPTER SIX

B y the time Jack Swartham returned to the inn, all was quiet. The many songs of Elvis were silent at the moment, while the impersonators slept, and when he walked into the room he shared with his wife, it smelled like a brewery. Lotta was snoring like a buzz saw, and Jack hoped he'd be able to get to sleep with all that noise. Slipping into his satin pajamas, he got into bed next to his unconscious wife and closed his eyes. The horrendous snoring droned on and on, giving him a headache. He tried pushing her, poking her, rolling her over, and nothing worked.

Furious, he flung the covers back and opened the drawer in his nightstand, looking for his ever-handy bottle of ibuprofen. Irritated when it wasn't there, he figured that Lotta must have used it before she passed out, and he stomped into the bathroom, the bright light stinging his sleep-deprived eyes. He found the bottle of ibuprofen on the ledge of the sink and popped two in his mouth, scooping up handfuls of tap water to swallow them with.

The snoring went on and on, not changing in volume or tone, but eventually, as his headache began to subside he relaxed, and finally, he went to sleep, plotting how he'd get back at Lotta in the morning by making as much noise as possible when he rose at his normal early hour. As he slipped over the edge into sleep, a fleeting thought passed through his brain. Why had Lotta been out drinking alone? She never did that.

**

Britney Lancer was tired, but euphoric after a wonderful rehearsal with Jack, and the cup of coffee they'd had afterward, in the hotel lobby, where they'd gloated over the fact that kept getting better and better and were going to sweep the awards at yet another convention, had made her forget all about her little tiff with Rocko. She slipped her card into the slot next to the door, trying not to make too much noise, so she wouldn't wake her husband, and was astounded to find all the lights in the room on, and no sign of Rocko.

"Rock?" she said quietly, walking slowly through the living area. "You sleepin'?"

She made her way to the bedroom, where the bed was untouched, and figured that her husband must be in the bathroom. The door was open a crack and it swung open when she knocked lightly, revealing that Rocko wasn't inside. Puzzled, she went back out to the living area to look for a note. She didn't see so much as a slip of paper letting her know where he might be, and this was very strange behavior for him. Had she finally pushed him too far? Had he left her? Rushing to the closet, she flung it open and saw that his suitcase was still there and his Elvis clothes were hanging where he'd left them, which made her sigh with relief. Rocko might leave her, but he'd never leave his costumes behind, so she knew he'd eventually be back from wherever he was.

Now that she was no longer worried about what was happening with her husband, she allowed herself to be frustrated that he'd made her worry. How utterly rude and inconsiderate of him! She got undressed, slipped into the non-sexiest long nightgown that she could find, turned out all the lights and left her shoes where he just might trip over them before flopping down into the bed and falling instantly asleep.

**

Rocko Lancer came to with his face pressed against the rough brick of a building. He had no idea where he was, or how he'd gotten there, but he did know that he had a throbbing headache and that the sun's rays were searing his retinas. He hadn't been this hungover in a very long time. He needed water, badly. His mouth felt like a desert and a smelly desert at that. His stomach sloshed uncomfortably when he moved, and blinding pain shot across his brow. His first order of business was hydration, because he couldn't even think about finding his way back to the hotel until he got some water in him and could think straight.

He got to his knees, and slowly made his way to a standing position, placing a hand on the wall to brace himself as the wave of nausea rocketed through him. He swallowed convulsively, keeping his eyes closed until the moment passed, then carefully turned his head right and left, taking in his surroundings. The area looked somehow familiar, and there seemed to be major roads off of both ends of the alley that he was in, so he headed toward the closest one.

Coming around the side of the building, he saw the delivery entrance for the hotel at which he was staying. It would seem that he'd almost made it back last night, and had passed out in the alley behind his own hotel. Two young men were unloading boxes from a van and were taking them into the hotel. They exchanged a knowing look as the rough-looking Elvis approached them.

"Hey, guys, any chance you could cut me a break and let me in the back way?" he asked, his own voice making his head throb.

One of the guys reached into the cab of the van and tossed him a sports drink.

"Here man, looks like you could use this."

"Sure, come on in," the other one invited, holding the door for him as he sipped at the glorious lemon lime liquid. "Anything for the King," he joked.

"Thank you, thank you very much," the impression was weak, but it got a laugh out of the delivery guys.

Rocko took a service elevator up to the lobby level, then got into the regular elevator, hoping that he didn't smell too badly, and rode up to his room, his stomach lurching when the car whooshed to a halt. Thankfully, he still had a watch to check, and when he glanced at it, after letting himself into the room, he noticed that it was Britney's breakfast time, so she must be at the breakfast bar of the hotel. Good. He could hydrate, shower and shave before he had to deal with her. He wasn't looking forward to their next conversation, and knew quite well that it might be their last.

CHAPTER SEVEN

S pencer Bengal's heart pounded in his chest, and he was second-guessing himself all over the place as he stood on Izzy Gilmore's doorstep, contemplating ringing the bell. Izzy was one of the top horror writers in the world, and had been Spencer's girlfriend for a short time several months ago. When he'd been working covertly for the Beckett family, and as a government operative, he'd been unable to share the details of his job with her, and she'd rejected him more than once when he'd reached out to her. She'd finally come around and wanted to have a relationship with him, once he was freed from his government obligation, but her reaction was a little too late. The veteran hadn't been able to trust her when he needed her most, and when she'd come back, yearning to be with him, he'd had to push her away.

He didn't know what he was doing standing there on her porch, and he'd turned to go more than once, but like a moth to a flame, he took a deep breath and rang the bell. Hercules, Izzy's giant Leonberger, woofed a couple of times, and Spencer could hear his nails clicking on the tile floor as he paced in front of the door, waiting for Izzy to open it. The gentle giant loved Spencer, and the feeling was entirely mutual.

Izzy opened the door looking absolutely adorable. Her mahogany tresses were tossed up into a messy bun, and she was wearing her standard "don't bother me, I'm writing," uniform of yoga pants and a bright pink tank top.

"Oh! Spence…hi," her eyebrows shot up her forehead in surprise, and color rose in her cheeks. "Is everything okay?"

The Marine stared at her, taking her in from head to toe, and was momentarily speechless.

"Uh, yeah…yes. Everything's fine. I was hoping that you might want to go for a walk with Herc or something, but it looks like you're busy, so," he turned to go, kicking himself for dropping by unannounced. Of course she was busy. She was a writer, she worked all the time.

"Hey, no, come back!" she called after him.

He turned slowly, halfway down the sidewalk.

"I…uh…I could use some fresh air, and poor Herc is feeling neglected," she assured him. Herc forced his head out between her leg and the door jamb, and when he saw Spencer, he practically bowled Izzy over to get to him.

Spencer squatted down and let the furry projectile tackle him, laughing with delight as they rolled to the ground in a firestorm of fur and slobber.

"Well, I guess that settles that," Spencer replied, wrestling with the dog playfully.

"Let me get a ball and some water for him, and we can walk to the park," Izzy disappeared into the house.

The trio had a lovely walk and played with Herc for about an hour before he decided to flop down for a nap under a tree.

"I think we wore him out," Izzy chuckled and scratched between the dog's ears.

"He's a good boy. I miss having a dog, but Moose is pretty awesome," Spencer watched her, thinking how amazing she looked with flushed cheeks and messy hair.

"Moose thinks he runs the house," Izzy grinned. "He's a pretty independent kitty."

"True story. Which is a good thing, considering that I'm almost never home anymore."

"How are you liking working for Chas?" Izzy leaned back against the trunk of the tree, next to Herc, who was now fast asleep.

"It's good. Things are really slow right now, because Chas is still working part-time for Calgon PD until they find his replacement, and he's not advertising for new cases until he's completely freed up, so we're dabbling in some cold cases and I'm supervising the overhaul of the house that they just bought."

"That sounds fun. I ran into Echo at the bookstore, and she told me that they'd finally found a place."

"It'll be really beautiful when all the work is done."

"I can't wait to see it."

"Well, once we get a little more ahead of the game, I'll give you a tour," Spencer picked a blade of grass and began tearing it into thin strips.

"Hey, Spence?"

"Yeah?"

"Why did you come over today?" Izzy asked softly, her hazel eyes warm.

Spencer sighed. "I missed you. And Herc. But mostly you," he admitted, his cobalt eyes locked on hers.

"Really?" her eyes widened.

"Really."

"I've been missing you for a long time," she murmured, glad to have Herc's soft fur as a distraction. She could run her fingers through it and use it as an excuse to mask her feelings by lowering her eyes.

"I know, and I'm sorry, Iz. It just took me a while to figure some things out."

"And have you?"

"Have I what?" he hedged, buying some time for the inevitable question that followed.

"Figured things out."

"Kinda," he picked another blade of grass.

"I don't know what that means."

"I don't either, actually, but what I do know is that it's silly if you're missing me, and I'm missing you, that we deny each other the pleasure of our company."

Izzy sat motionless, staring at the gorgeous young veteran. "What do you mean, Spence?" Her voice was practically a whisper.

"I mean, I think it's okay for us to start seeing each other again, with no pressure. We can just take each day as it comes and see what happens," he shrugged, looking up at her tentatively. "That is, if you still want to see me. I know you've got a lot going on and…oof!"

His sentence was cut off as Izzy launched herself into his arms, hugging him with all her might. Embarrassed at her own reaction, she sat back after they'd embraced.

"Sorry," she looked down, blushing.

"No apologies," Spencer chuckled. "Hugs are part of the bargain. I missed those, too."

"I'll try to control myself," she said a bit breathlessly, gazing into his eyes.

"You don't have to," he said softly.

SUMMER PRESCOTT

CHAPTER EIGHT

S pencer had loaded the last box of cupcakes into the Cupcakes in Paradise delivery van, and Missy was so thankful that he was still around to help her, despite staying busy with the new house and the investigation agency. They brought the cupcakes to the convention center, and were invited to watch the competition.

"You up for it?" Missy's excitement was obvious.

"Heck yeah, I'm an Elvis fan from way back," Spencer agreed.

The stage manager gave them VIP passes, which led them to prime seats in the front row. The crowd was large, but friendly, and folks were passing time before the show by bouncing beach balls around.

"This is going to be so fun," Missy grinned.

Spencer nodded, scanning the audience and doing surveillance without even realizing it. Old habits die hard.

**

"Jack...sweetie, are you okay?" Britney Lancer frowned at her partner.

His skin was sweaty and grey, and he'd run to the bathroom multiple times in the past half hour.

"I'll be fine," his voice was hoarse. "I took some stomach soothing pink stuff."

"You're breathing funny...are you going to be able to sing?"

"Heck yeah, doll. The show...must...go on," he wheezed. "We're next."

"Okay," she sighed, shaking her head. "But if you can't do this, you need to let me know now and I'll just do the act by myself. You look like you need a hospital," she squeezed his shoulder.

"No. Just flu. We got this," he shook his head, a patch of white spittle clinging to the corner of his mouth.

Their names were called just then, and Jack stiffened his spine, took some shallow breaths and strutted out onto the stage, with Britney on his arm. Their opening music thumped through the convention center, and Jack bounced his leg, Elvis-style, but suddenly seemed off balance. The color drained from his face, and just when he was supposed to start singing, he collapsed, his head making a loud thud as it hit the stage. Jack's body convulsed two or three times, then stilled as the paramedics who were on call for the event rushed to the stage. The curtains were closed, and roughly twenty minutes later, an event organizer stood before the hushed crowd. There were no bouncing beach balls as they waited for news as to what had transpired.

"Folks," the announcer's voice was grave. "Due to unforeseen circumstances, we've had to cancel tonight's show. We'll be rescheduling this show to five o'clock tomorrow, before the big event. I apologize for any inconvenience. If you'd rather have a refund, please go to our website. Thank you very much."

Missy looked at Spencer, alarmed.

"Oh my goodness, I wonder what happened to that poor man," she whispered.

"It can't be good," the Marine scanned the audience, and when he saw Chas slip in a side door, he knew there was trouble.

Missy saw her husband, too.

"Oh dear. Why don't you go and see if Chas needs anything?" she patted his arm. "I can drive the van home."

"Yes ma'am," he nodded, and wove his way through the exiting crowd, moving toward the stage.

"What do we have?" he asked in a low voice, when he reached his boss's side.

"Dead Elvis," Chas replied. "Coroner is on his way."

Spencer noticed a crowd of Elvis's standing behind the paramedics, as they blocked access to the body, along with one hysterical Marilyn Monroe

**

"Elvis is dead," mortuary assistant, Fiona McCamish announced, standing in the doorway of Timothy Eckels's office.

Tim was both the coroner for Calgon, and the owner of the only funeral home in town, so he ran both the morgue and the mortuary, and his spunky assistant Fiona picked up the slack whenever he was needed at one place or the other. The edgy assistant had begged and badgered Tim for a job until he relented, with one condition. She was required to get rid of her extreme hair, piercings and makeup, and dress professionally. To that end, Missy and Echo had taken her shopping and for a makeover, and in the end, a very attractive young woman who still retained her brash attitude had reported for work at the mortuary.

"He died years ago, actually," Tim mumbled, not looking up from the latest issue of Mortuary Monthly.

"Nope, he died about half an hour ago on the stage at the Convention Center," she waved a yellow sticky note at him.

That made her boss look up and blink rapidly from behind his coke bottle lensed glasses.

"Have you been sniffing the embalming fluids?" he deadpanned.

Fiona gave him a look and crossed her arms.

"There's an Elvis impersonator competition going on this weekend at the Convention Center. One of the Elvis's took a dive onstage and they're worried that he might have plague or something. The detective said he looked pretty bad."

That got Tim's attention and he closed his magazine, marking his page with a coffin brochure.

"Is the..." he reached for his lab coat.

"Yes, I put your bag in the car."

"Did you..."

"Yes, the doors are locked and the alarm is set."

"Are the..."

"Yup, the directions are entered in the GPS," Fiona sighed, knowing the routine, having gone through it seemingly hundreds of times.

"Well then, don't dilly-dally, we have a job to do," he groused, walking rapidly toward the garage.

Fiona rolled her eyes and trailed behind him.

"I'm driving," she said, with a mischievous gleam in her eyes.

"No, you're not."

"Aww…c'mon Timmy."

"Don't call me that."

As they pulled the hearse out of the mortuary's oversized driveway, Fiona felt a chill that raised the hairs on the back of her neck, almost like someone was watching them. She whipped her head around, scanning the immediate area, but seeing nothing. She thought she might have seen some movement behind a bush at the business next door, but it was probably just the wind. Shaking it off, she kicked back and enjoyed the ride to the Convention Center. It was good to get out of the cool, serene confines of the mortuary and out into the sunlight.

CHAPTER NINE

"Y ou want to talk to the wife or the girlfriend?" Chas asked Spencer, when Tim whisked Jack's body away to the morgue, having determined that an autopsy was indicated.

"Which one is Marilyn?" Spencer inclined his head toward the still-sobbing entertainer.

"The girlfriend, if the rumors are to be believed."

"Then I'll take the wife."

"Okay, you interview the wife and Marilyn's husband, and I'll interview Marilyn, er, Britney," Chas nodded, pointing out Lotta and Rocko. "No one involved with the show leaves here until we've taken statements from all of them."

"Gonna be a long night," Spencer remarked.

"I've got every uniform that Calgon PD can spare here to help out."

"Good call," the Marine said quietly before heading over to Lotta.

"Mrs. Swartham? I'm Spencer Bengal…I'm so sorry for your loss," Spencer said, extending his hand. When Lotta shook it, he held on and patted her hand with his left hand for a moment, oozing sincerity. "I know this is an awful time, but I need to have a little more information about your husband. Can we talk for a few minutes?"

Assuming that he was just an extremely good-looking cop, Lotta nodded and followed him backstage, where he found an empty dressing room in which they could talk. After inquiring gently about Jack's health, state of mind, schedule and other mundane things, Spencer leaned forward and began asking the real questions.

"Do you know of anyone who might have recently had an argument or disagreement with your husband?"

"Not that I know of," Lotta shrugged. "All the guys were jealous of Jacky, cuz he always won the competitions, so there coulda been a buncha guys who were mad at him."

"But no one in particular?"

"Not that I know of," Lotta rested her face in her hands and Spencer noticed that her eyes weren't red-rimmed or bloodshot.

People handled grief in their own ways, but he found it a bit peculiar that Jack's wife apparently hadn't shed a tear when her husband had convulsed and died on stage, his makeup melting from his face under the lights.

"Pardon me for asking, but...how was your marriage?"

Lotta stared at him for a moment and something flickered in her eyes.

"Not bad, not great," she said candidly.

"Do you think there's any possibility that your husband might have been unfaithful?"

"Yeah, I think he probably was. With that little tramp out there," she gestured toward the stage bitterly.

"Are you referring to his singing partner?"

"Yeah, they said that the Association of Impersonator Competitions chose who was partnered with who, but me and Rocko just found out last night that that ain't true at all. Jack and Britney chose each other. They had to get it approved in advance and everything," Lotta shook her head in disgust.

"And Rocko is...?"

"Britney's husband. A solid guy."

"You know him well?"

"He's been going head to head with Jack for years. Usually comes in second or third. Good guy. He deserves better than the likes of her," she grimaced.

"Mrs. Swartham, can you please recount for me what happened with you and Jack over the last twenty-four hours, that sort of thing? Was he acting strangely?"

"No stranger than usual when Britney's around. He told me the day before yesterday that he was gonna be practicing his act with her last night. Gave me some money and told me to get a nice dress for the awards. I didn't feel like shopping, so when he went to rehearsal, I followed him, just to watch. That's when I found out from the stage manager that he and Britney had been lying to me and Rocko the whole time. After we found out, me and Rock went out for drinks. Even though it was a sad night, we had a good time," she pursed her lips and nodded.

"A good time, meaning…?"

"Oh no, nothing like that. Jack and Britney may play loose and free like that, but I ain't made that way. I think Rocko would've been willing, but my heart wasn't in it, ya know. We just had drinks. Lots of em."

"Where did you go for drinks?"

"Someplace downtown. They had hanging lamps that were like clusters of grapes, kind of a groovy vibe."

"Ballard's?" Spencer guessed.

"Yeah, I think that was it."

"And what time did you leave?"

"I was getting pretty sleepy, so I left right around ten, I think, and took a cab back to the inn."

"The inn?"

"The Beach House B&B, that's where we're staying."

"I see. And where was Jack while you were out with Rocko?"

"He was still rehearsing. He puts in long nights of rehearsal the night before a show. I came in and went to bed. He wasn't home yet."

"Did he come back to the hotel at all?"

"Yeah, he came in sometime while I was asleep. He was there in the morning, making all kinds of noise, but he was in his pajamas, so I knew he'd slept there."

"And what was your morning like?"

"I yelled at him. I was mad because he lied to me about Britney."

"How did he react?"

"Told me I was crazy. Told me if I loved him, I'd respect his professionalism. It was ugly, and I ended up not talking to him. When I got out of the shower, he was gone to breakfast, and I left the inn early. We didn't speak again. I came backstage just before he was supposed to go on, and saw Rocko yellin' at him about something, so I just hung back. Then he went on stage and he collapsed."

"Did you happen to hear what Rocko said?"

Lotta snorted.

"No, but I can guess. He thought the world of Britney, and the thought of another man touching her…I'm sure he went through the roof."

"Do you know for a fact that they were having an affair? Did you see them together other than while they were working?

"Well no, but honey, lemme tell ya…a wife just knows."

CHAPTER TEN

Missy and Echo drove over to the new house to see what progress had been made, with Echo's precious baby Jasmine gurgling happily in the back seat. Spencer and Chas were off dealing with the witnesses to the Elvis death, Izzy had agreed to man the counter at Cupcakes in Paradise for a couple of hours, and Joyce Rutledge, the Ivy-League educated bookworm who managed the bookstore and candle shop that Echo owned in a funky retro building downtown, had things well under control so the new mama could take some time for herself.

After the friends checked out the house, they'd have lunch out and maybe even do a little shopping, depending upon Jasmine's cooperation.

"That must've been awful, seeing that man fall to the stage like that," Echo shook her head.

"Oh, I can't even begin to tell you. The sound that his head made when it hit the floor..." Missy shuddered, unable to even finish the sentence. "I felt so bad. I had no idea that he would die, I was hoping it was just nerves or something."

"Most of those impersonators do it for a living, they probably don't even get nervous after awhile."

"Hmm, I never thought of that. Well, here we are," Missy announced proudly, turning into her private lane.

"Wow, they really trimmed things back, you can actually get in the driveway without trees and shrubs scraping the car," Echo observed. "What a difference!"

Spencer's crew had been hard at work, and new stucco was being applied to the exterior, now that the roof and all of the windows had been replaced. Inside, the house had been basically stripped down to the studs, and some of the new drywall had already gone up, once the plumbing and electrical in certain sections had been updated.

"This is actually starting to look like a home again," Missy smiled.

"And a gorgeous one at that," Echo agreed, patting Jasmine's back as she slept soundly in her front pack.

The stairs were blocked, but they heard the sounds of construction activity taking place in the upstairs bedrooms and library.

"Let's go take a look at the pool and yard," Missy suggested, leading the way.

"As long as nothing crawls on me," Echo shivered.

"Don't worry, I'll protect you," Missy teased.

"Aww…thanks, I feel so much better now," Echo replied dryly, making a face.

The pool had been emptied, repaired and cleaned thoroughly, and new gunite was being applied to the surface, along with glass tiles on the sides. The brush and debris had been cleared from the huge back yard, and Missy held her hand up to her eyes to shield them from the sun as she looked into the distance.

"Hey, do you see that?" she nudged Echo.

"What?"

"Doesn't it look like there's a structure down there? Like a little house or something?"

"Now that you mention it, it does look like there's something behind those trees on the right," Echo nodded.

"You up for a walk?"

"What do you mean?"

"Let's go see what that building is. My curiosity is killing me," Missy grinned.

"Your curiosity is going to kill us both someday, but I'd rather that it wasn't today," Echo raised an eyebrow.

"When did you become such a chicken, girl? Where's your sense of adventure?" Missy teased.

"I'm not a chicken, I'm an adult," Echo stuck out her tongue. "Besides, I'm a mom now, I can't do risky things anymore."

"Oh no, you're not going to blame that precious baby for you being a scaredy-cat," Missy put her hands on her hips and tapped her foot.

"First I'm a chicken, now I'm a cat…I guess I'd better go with you before you turn me into a frog," Echo muttered.

"No worries, I haven't learned how to do magic…yet," Missy winked.

"Other than in the kitchen. The things I do for good vegan cupcakes," Echo complained trudging behind her best friend as they skirted the pool and headed out into the vast yard, making a beeline for the trees at the far end.

"Are we there yet?" Echo grunted, keeping up with Missy, but complaining in a good-natured way all the while.

"Of course we are. We're just walking for the joy of it now."

"That's why I'm feeling so joyful."

"Oh wow, check it out," Missy breathed as they came to the tree line.

"It's like a fairytale," Echo exclaimed, astonished.

A cottage that looked like it had once upon a time been inhabited by fairies and other mythical creatures stood tattered and abandoned behind the stand of trees. They could barely make out the outlines of what once had to have been meticulously tended gardens, and remnants of lace curtains still hung at the windows.

Echo started walking toward the door, carefully picking her way through the undergrowth. "Oh we are so going in there," she murmured.

"What happened to the fraidy cat?" Missy teased.

"I didn't walk this far to not see the inside of the fairytale cottage," Echo called back over her shoulder, not breaking stride.

"I'm with you on that one."

The door to the cottage was locked, but ajar, so they pushed hard and made it inside. While incredibly dusty and a bit dim, the inside of the cottage was a perfect little home with a kitchen, living room with a central fireplace, a dining area, two bedrooms and a bathroom that had a stunning claw foot tub, covered in dust and filled with debris.

"Am I dreaming?" Echo asked, turning slowly in circles, taking it all in.

"This is amazing," Missy beamed. "And I know just what to do with it."

"Film a movie?"

"No, silly. I'm going to offer it to Spencer. He won't be living in the basement apartment at the inn once Chas and I move out. He can have this place instead. I'll talk to the foreman about making it absolutely beautiful inside and out."

"That's a great idea. There's so much potential here," Echo agreed.

"I think finding this property may just be the best thing that could have happened for us right now."

"Sure seems like it. OH!" both women made a startled sound and nearly jumped out of their skins when the door to the cottage squeaked open, silhouetting a man in the doorway.

Putting a hand over her heart and chuckling, Missy spoke. "Hello, are you the foreman?"

The man, whose face they couldn't see in the dim light, stood stock still, not saying a word, then without uttering a sound, he turned and ran into the woods, disappearing before Missy could even catch a glimpse of him, though she had run out immediately.

"Hey!" she called out. "Who are you?" But her cries went unanswered.

"That was odd," Echo remarked, closing the door to the cottage behind her, as best she could.

"Yes, it was," Missy frowned. "Who was he, and what was he doing here?"

"I don't know, but if I were you, I'd have the workers put a lock on this door right away. You don't want someone to trash it before Spencer can get moved in."

"Good point," Missy nodded. "Let's get back and I'll let someone know. I wish I knew who that was," she murmured.

"Well, hopefully whoever it was doesn't come back."

"Yes, but why was he here in the first place?"

"Are you going to tell Chas about it?"

"Of course. Maybe he'll know something about the cottage. I think he got some of the history of the place from the city records."

"Maybe that'll give him an idea as to who it might be. Or, there's always the possibility that it was just someone passing through," Echo shrugged, causing Jasmine to stir a bit. The tender babe had slept through all of the excitement.

"Hopefully. Looks like we need to get a little girl her lunch," Missy observed with a tender smile.

"And then maybe I'll get to eat a warm meal," Echo kissed the top of Jasmine's downy head, inhaling her sweet fragrance.

CHAPTER ELEVEN

"This wasn't disease," Tim observed, his light shining down on the eviscerated shell of what was once Jack Swartham.

"How can you tell?" Fiona asked, shining her flashlight on his lungs and wondering why they looked funny, her breath hissing through her respirator.

"Cell death. Everywhere. All major systems shut down," Tim continued probing.

"Well, don't all systems shut down when someone dies anyhow?"

Tim paused his labor and stood up to stare at her, blinking with incredulity.

"It's different," he made a face which suggested that she should have known that, and returned to the task at hand.

Fiona had stuck like glue to Tim from the very beginning. Death in all its forms fascinated her, and she absorbed information from the highly skilled coroner like a sponge. Her goal was to learn everything that she could from him so that someday, he'd allow her to perform functions higher than handing him instruments and collecting specimens.

"This should confirm my suspicions," he mumbled, wielding his scalpel. "Yes, just as I thought."

"What, what is it? Why is there all that blood in his stomach?"

"Because he was poisoned. Take tissue samples from the areas and organs that I've listed here," he handed her the clipboard, "and make sure to take scrapings from under his fingernails, cheek swabs, and...swab for..." Tim cleared his throat, clearly uncomfortable.

"Extraneous DNA?" Fiona supplied, letting him off the hook. Her timid boss didn't want to reference acts of intimacy, but she'd known what he meant.

"Precisely," he turned away, snapping off his gloves. "I have reports to write. Let me know when you're done, I'll want to extract my own samples before sending them to the lab."

"You got it, Timmy," she grinned, and suddenly every light in the place went out.

Fiona was a tough girl, tougher than most in fact, and she'd weathered her share of storms, but feeling her way around the morgue in the dark, with a splayed open body on the table was not something that she was prepared to deal with.

"Tim?" her voice quavered just a bit, as she stood over Jack Swartham's corpse, a scalpel in one hand and a plastic specimen jar in the other.

She felt a hand on her shoulder and screamed, then slashed at the darkness with her scalpel.

"There's no need to carry on like that, it's just a power outage," Tim's glorious cantankerousness was like a beacon in the darkness, and, dropping the scalpel and the specimen jar, aiming for the sound of his voice, she flung her arms around his neck and held him tight, trembling slightly. Tim let her hang on for a brief moment before the voice of practicality once more cut through the darkness.

"If you'll kindly extricate yourself, I'll go check the fuse box," the coroner said calmly, his voice slightly muffled by her shoulder.

"Oh, yeah, sorry. I thought…you might be scared," Fiona muttered lamely and released her hold.

"Your kindness knows no bounds," was the droll reply as he made his way through the darkness as though he knew every nook and cranny in the place, which of course, he did.

Fiona stood alone in the dark, listening, straining for any sound, acutely aware of her vulnerability. Tim was taking forever, and she'd lost her bearings after she impulsively jumped into his arms. She didn't know where she was in the room, or even which direction she was facing. The morgue was in the basement of a city building, and without proper lighting, or the glow of various electronics, the place was, perhaps fittingly, like a tomb. Hearing footsteps on the stairs, her heart leapt to her throat.

"Tim?" she barely croaked out.

The footsteps stopped, then retreated, and now Fiona was even more freaked out than ever. She knelt down, hoping that whoever was out there might trip over her if they came down the stairs again. Hugging her midsection, she tucked her chin to her chest and tried her best to breathe normally. It was just her. Fiona. By herself. With what was once Jack Swartham.

After an eternity, the lights came back on and Fiona nearly fainted with relief. Moments later, Tim came trotting down the stairs.

"What happened?" Fiona demanded, tossing her dirty scalpel and specimen jar in the industrial sink beside the cold metal exam table.

Tim looked perplexed. "Oddly, the fuse box was missing a fuse. Fortunately, I always keep spares."

"Missing a fuse? How did that happen?" for some reason, goosebumps popped up all over Fiona's body. "Did it fall out or something?"

"No. Fuses do not fall out. It would seem that someone took it."

"Why would someone take a fuse? Are there other things that it can be used for?"

"No."

"Should we be worried about this?" Fiona licked her lips nervously.

"No."

"Are you going to call the police?"

Tim sighed and looked at her.

"No problem," she snapped off her gloves. "I'll definitely call them."

**

Rocko Lancer was drunk again, but this time it was Britney sitting with him at Ballard's, rather than Lotta Swartham.

"Couldn't happen to a nicer guy," he slurred, raising his glass and downing the contents, for the third time. Rocko had never been much of a drinker, but he'd found solace in the bottle twice this week…so far.

"You just stop that nasty talk right now," Britney scolded him, tearing up a bit. She'd been nursing the same gin and tonic since they arrived. "Jack was nice. He was my friend, and I wouldn't have won nearly as many competitions if it hadn't been for him, so you just knock it off," she demanded, her lips in a pretty pout.

"Yeah sure, you stick up for your boyfriend. Lousy backstabber. First he took my routines and my costume ideas, then he took my woman. I don't know who's worse, him or you. Good riddance. Karma snuck up on him and smacked him in the head and he deserved it," Rocko slammed his glass down on the bar. "Barkeep, gimme another," he shouted.

The bartender made his way over and stood in front of the couple.

"I'm sorry, sir, I'm not going to be able to serve you anymore," he leaned in and spoke quietly, the epitome of discretion.

"What the…? Why not?" Rocko blinked several times to clear his vision and squinted at his watch. "Iss only nine o'clock!"

"It's eleven thirty and I'm gonna have to ask you to take care of your tab and go," the bartender insisted.

"No!" Rocko shook his head and nearly fell from his barstool. "I ain't goin' nowhere. I'm gonna have another drink."

All during the conversation between the two men, Britney had been staring at her husband, and now her mouth dropped open in dawning horror.

Gripping his arm, she bared her teeth and leaned in, shouting in his face. "You did it, didn't you, Rock? You killed Jack Swartham. I don't know how you did it, but you did, didn't you?"

Rocko shook her off of his arm and turned toward the rest rooms, not bothering to reply. At the bartender's signal, the largest bouncer in the bar followed Rocko to the bathroom. Moments later a loud whump resounded behind the closed door of the men's room, followed by silence. Shortly after, the police arrived and took Britney and Rocko into custody. Britney was released shortly after arriving at the police station, with a stern warning about disturbing the peace, and Rocko was booked for public intoxication, disturbing the peace, and vandalism. Apparently, when he'd passed out in the bathroom, he'd knocked a paper towel dispenser off the wall with his shoulder. That was gonna hurt in the morning. So was his upcoming intense conversation with Chas Beckett.

CHAPTER TWELVE

B en Maribus had seen some pretty disturbing things in his adult life; it was kind of an occupational hazard. Bartenders pretty regularly got to hear sad life stories and witness all sorts of interpersonal conflict that often came as a result of lowered inhibitions, but last night's encounter with the impersonator couple had set off all sorts of inner alarms for him. Though the middle-aged bartender usually kept to himself, he felt that there was potentially enough at stake this time to force him out of his comfort zone. Ben had never been in a police station in his life, but he stood on the sidewalk outside the Calgon PD right now, working up the courage to go in. A uniformed cop walked up and held the door open for him, taking the choice out of his hands, so he mustered up the will and walked into the station.

"Help you?" the desk sergeant asked, looking up from his paperwork and seeming to assess him.

Though Ben had done nothing wrong, he inexplicably felt guilty.

"I, uh…I overheard a conversation last night that I think may be important."

The cop raised an eyebrow. "Care to elaborate?"

"Uh, yeah, sorry. I'm a bartender at Ballard's and this couple came in. They got it a fight and the wife kind of accused the husband of murder. The guy got taken away by you guys. He may still be here for all I know," Ben shrugged.

"Kind of accused him of murder."

"Yes," Ben nodded, feeling as though this had turned out to be a bad idea. The cop was skeptical and he was beginning to feel like an idiot.

"What's your name?" he asked, causing Ben's heart to drop to his feet.

"Ben. Ben Maribus."

"Have a seat," the cop ordered, glancing over at a bank of vinyl and metal chairs that were bolted to the floor.

"Look, if you think it's no big deal, I can just leave," Ben started backing toward the door.

"Have a seat," the desk sergeant gave him a look that brooked no nonsense.

Ben sat. The cop was only gone for a few minutes. When he came back, he was trailed by an intimidating guy in a flawless suit.

"Ben Maribus?" the lantern-jawed detective asked.

Suddenly it was difficult to swallow. "Yes," his answer sounded too eager. Too nervous, and he winced inwardly.

"Chas Beckett," the detective gave a perfunctory smile and extended his hand. Ben shook it. "Come with me, please."

Uh geez, I'm going to jail now, Ben thought irrationally and followed Chas down the hall to his office like a wayward puppy who was about to be scolded.

"Have a seat," the detective gestured to a chair across the desk from his executive one. Again, Ben sat. "So I understand that you may have some information about a murder?"

"Uh, yeah," Ben swallowed and nodded, then related to Chas what had happened at the bar.

"Did you hear what their names were?"

"No, but I have his credit card imprint," he dug into his pocket and handed the slip over to Chas, who raised his eyebrows when he read the name.

"Good work."

"Thanks."

Before Chas could ask another question, the desk sergeant knocked on his door again, opening it.

"Sorry to interrupt," the cop sighed. "We got another one out here talking about murder. A woman this time."

"Blonde?" Chas asked.

"Yeah, looks like Marilyn Monroe."

"Mr. Maribus, thank you for your time. If you remember anything else about this couple or anything that they might have said or done last night, please call me as soon as possible," Chas handed Ben a card.

"So I can go?"

"Yes, thanks for your time, we're done here," Chas shook his hand and left the room. Ben followed, with the desk sergeant bringing up the rear.

Britney Lancer gave the bartender a long look as he passed her on his way out, and Ben kept his eyes on the door.

Chas introduced himself, and moments later, the buxom blonde sat where Ben had been sitting.

"You have possible information about a murder?" the detective asked, and immediately, Britney Lancer burst into tears. From what he'd witnessed at the convention center, it was something that came easily to her. He handed her a tissue and waited for her to compose herself.

"I hate this," she whispered, dabbing underneath her eyes to make certain that her waterproof mascara was doing its job.

"Take your time," Chas encouraged, leaning back in his chair. He'd already interviewed Britney once, and wondered what new information she might have.

"I think…" she began, then choked up and shook her head. Taking a few deep shuddering breaths, she tried again.

"I think my husband may have had something to do with Jack's death," she blurted finally, the waterworks beginning again.

Chas showed no outward reaction.

"What makes you say that, Britney?" he leaned forward, interlacing his fingers in front of him on the desk.

"He's always been jealous of him," she whispered. "He says that Jack stole his costume designs, but Jack always spent way more money to make his costumes look authentic, and Rock hated that Jack and I always sang together so that we could win the competitions," she confessed.

"So, why didn't you just sing with your husband?"

"I feel like such a schlep saying this, but…"

"Go on," Chas encouraged.

"Rocko just wasn't as good as Jack in performance. He didn't have the curled lip down right, and he couldn't hit all of the notes. Jack had a much bigger range. I'd rather get half the prize money than perform with Rock and get nothing. Is that awful?"

"It makes complete sense from a business standpoint," Chas said neutrally. "Why do you think your husband might be involved?"

"He wasn't in our hotel room when I got back from rehearsal, and I don't know where he went. He usually came in second place in the competitions, so if Jack wasn't around…" she let the sentence trail off, then leaned over the desk toward Chas. "And there's more…"

"Oh?"

"Yeah. This is really embarrassing, but Rocko thought that Jack and I were…you know," she blushed and looked down at the desk.

"Were what?" Chas asked, knowing full well what she meant.

"Having an affair," she mumbled, not looking at him.

"Were you?" he asked mildly.

"No!" she shook her head vehemently. "I mean, if I'm being honest, I thought about it sometimes, but Jack was married, and I'm married, and it just wouldn't be right, you know."

"Did your husband confront you about his suspicions?"

"Did he ever! Like every time me and Jack sang together," she rolled her eyes, an expression that looked more than incongruent with her tear-stained cheeks.

"Had he mentioned it recently?"

"Yep, right before rehearsal. Right before he disappeared for the night."

"How's your marriage?" Chas asked quietly, the soul of compassion.

"It's good. I don't want Rock to go to jail, I love him and he loves me, but if he's done something awful, I just thought that somebody should know," she started to cry. "When we were at the bar, he basically said that Jack deserved to die. He wasn't freaked out about it at all, it was awful," she shook her head and dabbed at her eyes again.

"Was your husband good friends with Lotta Swartham?"

That made Britney pause and stare at the detective for a moment.

"Good friends? No, I wouldn't say that. They knew each other from the competitions…sometimes they sat together when me and Jack were performing, but, I wouldn't say they were friends."

"What about you and Lotta? Are you friends?"

Britney shook her head and looked down at the desk. "No, I don't think she liked me very much."

"Why is that?"

"I don't know. She's…older you know, and I spent a lot of time with Jack, rehearsing and stuff," she shrugged. "Maybe she was jealous or something, I don't know. Why? Do you think that she had something to do with Jack's death?"

"I have to explore all possibilities."

"Okay," she nodded. "I think that's about all I have to say. Would it be okay if I left now?" she asked, seeming tired, probably drained from crying.

"Of course. If you think of anything else that might be helpful, just give me a call."

"Thank you so much, Detective. It wasn't easy to come down here today, but you're a real good listener."

"Comes with the territory," Chas smiled and stood to show her out of the office. After walking her to the door, he headed for the holding cells, eager to get Rocko Lancer into an interrogation room.

SUMMER PRESCOTT

CHAPTER THIRTEEN

After breakfast at the inn, which Lotta Swartham pushed around on her plate, only nibbling at occasionally, the widow took a taxi to the mall to do some shopping, which Missy found a bit odd, but she tried to never judge people's coping mechanisms. Most of the other Elvises had checked out of the inn yesterday, after the competition was won by a complete newcomer from Colorado, but Lotta had stayed, at the request of the Calgon PD, while they waited to determine whether or not foul play had been involved in her husband's death.

Missy and Echo sat in the Wedgewood parlor of the inn, sipping tea after helping Maggie, the ever-efficient innkeeper serve breakfast. Since Missy and Chas couldn't move into their new home yet, Carla hadn't taken over the Owner's Quarters, and often didn't arrive at the inn until nearly lunch time.

"You know what I would love," Echo mused.

"What's that?"

"I'd love to see all of the Elvis costumes that these guys have. I just think it would be fascinating. I love vintage fashion, as you know."

"Yeah, it is interesting," Missy nodded. "Hey, there might be a way that we could see at least some of them," she got a devilish gleam in her eye.

"Oh?" Echo sat up and put down her tea.

"If Maggie needs help tidying the rooms, we could tell her that we'll clean up the Swartham's. I think all of the Elvis costumes that the poor man used are still hanging in the closet."

"Ohhhh…I never even thought of that. It's brilliant, do you think she'll go for it?"

"Hmm…let me think. Taking some work off of her hands while she's trying to recover from Elvis weekend and get Carla trained at the same time…yeah, I think she'll be okay with it," Missy teased.

"Okay, let's go ask for the key."

The two women, feeling quite clever and just a bit naughty, let themselves in to the Swartham's room and were astounded by the mess. Clothing, snacks and empty fast food wrappers covered every surface, the bed was unmade, and there were towels thrown on the bathroom floor.

"Wow, I get that she's grieving, but this woman certainly isn't much of a housekeeper," Echo made a face.

"No wonder she didn't eat much breakfast," Missy observed, swiping a half-eaten slice of pizza off of a nightstand and into a trash can.

"Ugh, I suppose we have to clean, since that's the excuse we used with Maggie," Echo wandered around the room, surveying the mess.

"Yes, we do. But let's see the costumes first."

"Agreed."

They went to the closet and Missy opened the door.

"Wow," Echo breathed. "Jackpot. No pun intended."

There were leather costumes, glittering jumpsuits which were painstakingly embellished with colorful rhinestones, military costumes, and even a jailhouse costume, each so authentic that they looked as though they had come from the closet of the King himself.

"Oh my goodness," Missy gasped. "They look just like they came from Graceland."

"You've been to Graceland?" Echo was surprised.

"Twice, and I'll be going again. You haven't?" Missy blinked at her.

"It's on my list."

They looked through the costumes for several minutes, then reluctantly shut the closet door and tackled the messy room. Once everything had been thrown out, folded up and removed from the floor, Echo made a bargain with Missy.

"I'll vacuum if you wipe down the bathroom."

"Fair enough," Missy nodded, arming herself with a bottle of disinfectant cleanser.

Echo ran the vacuum along the side of the bed, getting as far underneath as she could, when the machine started making a terrible racket.

"Oh geez," she muttered, turning it off.

"Everything okay out there?" Missy called from the bathroom.

"Yes, it's fine. I think I just sucked up a corner of a sheet or something," she replied, getting down on all fours to check the head of the vacuum.

When she flipped the attachment over, she saw that she'd accidentally sucked up a little plastic baggie. Pulling on the end of it, she saw its strange contents and called for Missy.

"Hey girl, you might want to come take a look at this," she called as she held it gingerly by one corner.

**

Fiona McCamish was troubled, and that was significant. Usually it took something big to rattle her cage. She typically handled whatever adversity that life threw her way with pragmatic calm, but she'd been on edge lately, so much so that she felt compelled to speak with her introverted boss about it.

"Hey, boss man, can I talk to you for a sec?" she asked, appearing in his office doorway with a manila folder in her hand.

Tim looked up from his computer and blinked at her, almost as if he'd been so into whatever he was doing that he hadn't heard her. That sort of thing happened all the time.

"Do you have a minute?" she asked again.

"I was reading about accelerated tissue degeneration," he commented.

"Oh good, so you're interruptible," she breezed in and flopped down in a chair across from him, not giving him the option of putting her off.

"What's that?" he asked, looking pointedly at the folder in her hand.

"The Swartham report. Stuff came in from the lab today," she said absently, her mind quite obviously elsewhere.

He stared at her, obviously expecting her to hand over the reports.

"You ever feel like someone is watching you?" she asked, baffling him. "Like there's this…I don't know…darkness following you around."

"Have you been sniffing the embalming fluid?" he blinked at her.

"No, I'm serious. You need to pay attention. I think we're being followed."

Tim and Fiona had recently become next door neighbors and carpooled back and forth to work.

"That's ridiculous, give me the report," he held out his hand, which she ignored.

"It's not ridiculous. I'm serious."

Tim sighed heavily and let his hand drop to the desk. "What makes you think that someone is following us? Have you seen something specific?" he frowned, clearly not convinced.

"Just little things, like bushes moving, and shadows where there shouldn't be any shadows…and then there was the "lights out" thing at the morgue," she pointed out.

"Bushes move in the wind, shadows can be caused by clouds moving over the sun, but, yes, the missing fuse was rather strange. I'll give you that," he conceded.

"Do you have any enemies?" Fiona asked, wracking her brain for solutions.

"While no one particularly likes me, I'm unaware of anyone who actively wishes me ill," he mused.

"Aww...you underestimate your own charm, Timmy. I like you."

"Don't call me that," was the automatic reply. "What about you? Enemies?"

"Well, I had a rough past, but I don't think there'd be anyone stalking me because of it. Steve hates me, but he's too dimwitted to be a threat."

"Loud Steve?" Tim raised an eyebrow.

Fiona had recently moved next door to Tim, she was renting the cute little home which belonged to Echo before she and Kel married. On the other side of her, lived her late sister's ex-husband, Steve, who was nicknamed Loud Steve because of his propensity to blare music from the overtaxed speakers in his small pickup truck. The neighbors could hear him coming from blocks away.

"Yeah, he used to be married to my sister, remember?"

"Yes, I do recall that. Hers was one of my first funerals in Calgon. Why does he hate you?"

"Because I always saw through him. He was an awful husband and my sister deserved better."

"And I suppose you had no problem telling him so."

"Of course not. I let him have it every time I saw him, but there's no way he'd be smart or careful enough to be following us."

"Then it's obviously a mere figment of your imagination."

"No, it's not," Fiona insisted.

"Perhaps we should drive separately for a while to determine if there is someone following you. Or me, for that matter."

"Definitely not," Fiona shook her head. "We're more vulnerable by ourselves."

Tim stared at her for a moment and sighed. His assistant, who was known for being bold and brash, was not typically given to fits of hysteria, so there was a slight chance that she wasn't imagining whatever was going on.

"Fine, we'll continue to carpool, and I'll attempt to be more aware of my surroundings. Now can I have the report?" he raised his eyebrows to indicate that it wasn't really a question.

"Oh, yeah." Fiona had forgotten that she still held it, and handed it over, watching her boss as he read it.

There was something rather comforting about the presence of the serious and socially awkward coroner. With his thinning hair, pale skin, thick glasses and dad bod, he wasn't what hardly anyone would call conventionally attractive, but for some reason, Fiona had always felt oddly drawn to him, despite their age difference.

Feeling her continued presence, he lowered the report and blinked at her.

"Was there something else that you needed?" he asked, sounding mildly annoyed.

"Oh, uh, no." She got up and left his office, head down, and he watched her go.

CHAPTER FOURTEEN

Izzy's heart pounded in her chest as she parked in front of Missy and Chas's new home-in-progress. She was surprising Spencer with a picnic lunch and hoped that he wouldn't mind. Opening the back door, she let Hercules out, then went behind the car to grab the picnic supplies. She'd spent so much time working with the massive dog that a leash wasn't necessary, he'd heel without being told, so both hands were free to carry her picnic basket, blanket and cooler.

"Wow, man. Lookit that dog!" she heard one of the workers exclaim and she had to grin to herself. Hercules always elicited some sort of reaction from folks who hadn't met him before.

"Whoa, I bet nobody messes with that chick," another chimed in, almost making Izzy laugh aloud.

Closing the trunk, she hit the button on her keys to lock the car, and started toward the house.

"Hello," she peered up at a worker who was on top of a ladder, installing a glass transom above the front door. "I'm looking for Spencer Bengal."

"Lucky man," the guy grinned. "Last I heard, he was out back, checking on the cabana renovation."

"Should I go through the house?"

"It's probably safer for the pads on that big guy's feet if you use the side yard. There's less chance of him stepping on a nail or construction materials," the pleasant young man advised.

"Great, thanks," she smiled and set off in the direction that he'd indicated, well aware of his appreciative stare as she walked away.

Hercules spotted Spencer before Izzy did, and with a low, friendly woof, he bounded over to where the Marine stood, going over plans with the construction foreman.

"Hey, buddy," Spencer grinned as the giant bundle of fur leapt up, putting both paws on his shoulders for a hug.

"Wow, that's quite an animal," the foreman stepped back, hoping that the dog was friendly to strangers.

"This is Hercules," Spencer answered, rubbing the dog's ears. "Hey Iz, what brings you down here?" he greeted her with a smile.

"Lunch," she held up the picnic basket. "Are you free?"

"As a bird," he replied, then turned to the foreman. "We'll finish this up in about an hour if that's alright with you."

"No problem. The guys have enough to keep them going for quite some time, so no rush. I just want to get the materials ordered as soon as I can. Enjoy your lunch."

As the foreman trotted toward the house, Hercules had a strange reaction, staring at him and growling low in his throat.

"Herc, no no," Izzy scolded, silencing the dog instantly. Spencer distracted him by scratching between his ears, and all was well. "He does that sometimes. He's just being protective I think."

"Good quality in a dog. I have someplace special to take you," his dimples made her heart beat faster. "Here, let me take those," he grabbed the cooler, blanket and basket, and set off toward the far end of the yard.

"Did you actually cook?" Spencer teased, knowing that Izzy wasn't exactly the most domestic person on the planet.

The author snorted. "Are you kidding? I went into the picnic section of idontcook.com."

"That's a thing?"

"Not only is that a thing, it's a fabulous thing that I use regularly. They deliver."

"You realize that I would've been fine with a hotdog from the gas station, right?"

"If you want to abuse your body like that, you can do it on your own time, buster. You're not subsisting on gas station fare on my watch," Izzy grinned, enjoying the site of Hercules trundling along beside Spencer. "Where are we going?"

"There's something cool that I found out here a few days ago."

"You're really enjoying this project, aren't you?"

"It keeps me busy until we get the agency up and running. Chas is still working part time for the Homicide Division, so, until they find his replacement, I'll have plenty of time to focus on getting his house ready."

"How's the inside coming?"

"It's amazing. The place is going to be perfect for them, grand but cozy."

They were approaching the tree line when Hercules stopped suddenly, his hackles rising. He lowered his head and began to growl low in his throat.

"Herc…" Izzy started to say, but stopped when Spencer, who had put down the picnic supplies, raised his hand and put a finger to his lips to signal her to be quiet.

He commanded Hercules to stay, in a voice so low that only the dog could hear it, and disappeared into the trees, heading for a small structure. Izzy moved forward a bit and Hercules jumped at the sound of her footstep.

"It's okay, big boy," she whispered in his ear, crouching next to him.

Minutes later, Spencer came walking out through the trees.

"It's okay, someone has been here, but we must have spooked them," he grimaced.

"Is everything okay? What is that place?" Izzy tried to get a better view through the trees.

"Come on back, I'll show it to you. It used to be a guest cottage, and Missy had a lock put on it until the guys could renovate it. Someone tore the lock right out of the wood, went in and totally trashed the place. Looks to me like they were looking for something."

"What could they have been looking for?"

"I have a few ideas. Chas has me looking into the history of the property," he said, stepping through a final line of trees, where the cottage came into full view.

The door was ruined, splintered beneath the lock, but Izzy still saw the charm.

"Oh wow, it's so cute. It looks like elves should live there," she smiled.

"I'm afraid the inside isn't cute at all right now," Spencer replied grimly, standing back to allow her to enter.

The walls had been torn down to the studs, the floorboards had been pried up and cabinets were ripped from the walls.

"Oh my," Izzy shook her head.

"Yeah, this is going to take some work to put back together."

"Look at it like a blank canvas," she squeezed his bicep then leaned her head against him.

"Always an optimist, aren't you?" he asked, admiration coloring his tone.

"It's gotten me this far. Now how about that picnic?"

CHAPTER FIFTEEN

E cho had been wrestling with her conscience ever since she and Missy had cleaned the Swartham's room at the inn, and when she could take it no longer, she drove downtown with Jasmine to see Chas.

"What a nice surprise," the detective commented when he came out to the reception area at the police station.

The first thing he did was reach for the baby. He took her in his arms, smiling down at her sweet pink face and was rewarded with a happy chortle.

"You do have a way with the ladies, Chas Beckett," Echo teased.

"Only the ones that are this age," he grinned, leading the way to his office and speaking softly to Jasmine.

"Oh, I don't know, Missy seems pretty taken with you."

"I sure hope so. I'm definitely the lucky one in that relationship."

"I think it's mutual," Echo sat down on the sofa in the corner of his office, and he sank into a wing-back chair next to it.

"So to what do I owe the pleasure of this precious company?" he was spellbound by the baby.

Echo sighed. "Well, it's probably nothing, but…"

"I've heard that more than once today, but I know that if you took the time to come down here, it's probably something," Chas encouraged.

"I hope not, but…okay. So, Missy and I were helping Maggie out at the inn…"

"And you snooped through the Elvis outfits. I know, my mischievous beloved told me," he chuckled, delighted that Jasmine had taken hold of his index finger and was gripping it tightly.

"Well, yes, but that's not it."

Chas noticed that Echo seemed worried, and sobered a bit. "What is it?"

"I found something while we were cleaning. I sucked it up in the vacuum actually, and it has me worried," she admitted.

"What did you find?" Chas moved Jasmine up to his shoulder and she snuggled into his neck.

"Castor beans."

"Castor beans?" his eyebrows shot skyward. "Are you sure?"

"Positive. I used to make poultices with them. They're great for skin infections."

"As much as I hate to give this little lady up, I have to make a phone call," the detective handed a sleepy Jasmine to her mother and pulled out his cell.

Hitting one of the buttons for speed dial, he waited impatiently for an answer.

"Eckels, Chas Beckett here. Do you happen to have the autopsy report for Jack Swartham back yet?"

He listened, nodding.

"Great, can I come by in about ten minutes to pick them up? Perfect. See you in a few."

The detective hung up and looked apologetically at Echo.

"No worries," she smiled and gave him a hug. "Duty calls, I get it. Little miss and I will just be on our way. Thanks for listening."

"Always a pleasure, and by the way…you may have just broken this case wide open."

He walked a stunned Echo to the door and they went their separate ways once they hit the sidewalk.

**

Chas sat across the interrogation table from Rocko Lancer, armed with the coroner's report.

"Were you having an affair with Lotta Swartham?" he asked without preamble.

Rocko squirmed uncomfortably. "It gets lonely on the road, ya know? Jack and Brit were always together, and I got left in the room. A lot. Lotta is a good woman," he shrugged, staring down at his hands.

"Were you two together here in Calgon?"

"Not in the carnal sense, if that's what you mean. The only time I was away from Brit is when I got rip-roaring drunk, the day before Jack died."

"Your wife said that you were glad he was dead."

"Brit said that?"

"Yes, and the bartender verified it."

"I didn't mean nothing by it. I was just feeling low, that's all."

"So you're trying to tell me that you didn't kill Jack so that you could be with Lotta and win the competitions?"

"No! I told you before, I didn't kill him. I think he was just sick or something."

"Maybe Lotta killed him to be with you."

"Nope," Rocko shook his head vehemently. "She might not have a happy marriage, but she's good people. She wouldn't do nothing like that."

"Does she like to garden?" Chas asked, out of the blue.

The question took Rocko entirely by surprise. He stared at the detective bug-eyed for a moment before answering.

"Lotta? They live in a condo, she couldn't garden if she wanted to. I don't think she even had house plants cuz they're gone so much. What difference does it make?"

"You live in a condo?"

"No. We got a house that's kinda in the country. Big back yard. My neighbor mows for us when we're gone."

"Does your wife have a green thumb?"

"Oh yeah. Brit loves plants. She can grow just about anything."

"You ever see her harvest these?" Chas shook the bag of beans that he'd found under Lotta's bed and tossed them down on the table.

"Oh yeah, she works with those things, makes stuff out of 'em."

"What kind of stuff?"

"Some kind of paste for like cuts and burns and pimples and stuff, and a powder that I think she uses to keep the mice outta the basement."

"Powder?"

"Yeah."

"White powder?"

"Yep."

"You know, Rocko, I don't really think we need to hold you here anymore. Do you have a ride home?"

"Yeah. Brit said to let her know when you released me so that she could come get me."

"I'll give her a call while you're getting processed out, so she can be here when you're ready," Chas offered.

"Mighty nice of you," Rocko looked at the detective like he'd grown a second head.

"Calgon PD is known for its courtesy," Chas rose. "Just sit tight, I'll have an officer bring you some paperwork."

"Alright," Rocko nodded, surprised at his sudden good fortune. "Hey, Detective," he called as Chas reached the door.

"Yes?"

"Thanks."

"Don't thank me yet," the detective quipped.

He left the interrogation room and made a quick call to Spencer.

"Meet me at the station as quickly as you can. Bring the stuff that you dug up on Jack Swartham. I'm going to stop by the evidence room, then I'll be in my office."

CHAPTER SIXTEEN

Rocko Lancer was shocked when his wife arrived at the police station to pick him up and was immediately arrested for the murder of Jack Swartham. Chas sat across from the defiant entertainer who looked like a very angry Marilyn Monroe.

"This is ridiculous, I loved Jack. I certainly wouldn't have killed him. I'd bet you anything that it's that neurotic wife of his. She nagged at him all the time. They fought like cats and dogs."

"Last time you were here talking to me, you were positive that your husband had killed him. What changed your mind?"

"It just seems like she'd be the one," Britney said lamely, crossing her arms.

"You know, I find it interesting that you came in here saying that Jack had been killed by your husband when speculation was that he'd actually died of a disease. Why did you think he'd been murdered, before anyone else did?"

"It just…it was so sudden. People don't come down with diseases all of a sudden like that."

"Could've been a heart attack, brain aneurysm, any number of medical problems, yet your mind automatically leaped to murder. Must have been because you were the only one who knew he'd been murdered," Chas suggested.

"I did not!"

"Yet you came down here to tell me that you thought you did," he raised an eyebrow. "Do you recognize these?" he asked, tossing the bag of castor beans on the table. They'd been recovered from the inn by a uniformed cop after Echo told Chas that they were there.

"Gonna grow a beanstalk?" she asked, voice dripping with sarcasm.

"This bag had your fingerprints all over it, and none of Lotta's."

"I've never seen it before in my life," she insisted, nervously chewing the inside of her cheek.

"How about this?" Chas held up another evidence bag containing the bottle of ibuprofen that Jack had gone to when he'd had his headache.

"I'm fine, thank you," she couldn't even muster up a good sarcastic tone this time, her voice wobbled.

"It also had your fingerprints all over it, and the tablets inside were lightly sprinkled with a fine dusting of white powder."

"Jack had headaches," she murmured.

"You know what that white dust is, Britney?" Chas drove the point home.

"Ricin," she whispered.

"Ricin," he tossed the bottle aside. "You poisoned Jack's ibuprofen because you knew that he usually had headaches after a long rehearsal. If the ricin killed him the morning of the show, you could do your act with your husband and win.

"I didn't kill Jack," she shook her head, tears rolling down her cheeks. "Why would I do that?"

Spencer stepped forward with a file folder of documents in his hand.

"Maybe because you and he had bought some property together with your winnings, and signed a contract that if something happened to the other person, the survivor would retain ownership, rather than having it pass to a spouse?" he tossed one document on the table.

"Or, it could be that you'd taken insurance out on him, claiming that it would have a negative impact on your career if he died," Spencer tossed another document down, making Britney wince.

"How much did you get out of that policy?" Chas asked, his eyes boring into hers.

"Half a million," she whispered.

"And where was the property?" he persisted.

"Belize. We were going to retire there."

"And I'm guessing that Rocko and Lotta had no idea."

"They had their own thing going on, and Jack knew it, but he still didn't divorce her," Britney swiped away bitter tears.

"Seems to me that you'd want to kill Lotta more than Jack. Were those tablets meant for her?"

"No. I knew that she didn't take over the counter meds. If I couldn't have him, she couldn't either. I just wanted to get my money and retire in Belize."

"So you made Ricin from the castor beans that you grew in your back yard, poisoned your lover and tried to frame his wife for it by tossing some of the beans under the bed in their room, is that about right?" Chas summed up.

Britney stared straight ahead, then burst into tears and dropped her head onto the table top.

"Put her in holding," the detective told the uniformed officer in the back of the room.

Chas and Spencer left the room.

"Good work," the detective clapped Spencer on the back.

"Thanks. I gotta admit, I didn't see that one coming. I figured Rocko and the wife had collaborated on it."

"Me, too. Guess you can't judge a book by its cover."

"Guess not."

"Well, I'm headed off to paperwork purgatory."

"Good luck with that," Spencer chuckled. "I have a date."

"Oh?"

"Yeah, Izzy and I are going to a movie."

"Really? So that's back on?"

"We'll see. We're taking things slowly."

"She's a great gal, if you want my two cents."

"Oh, I'm fully aware, but thanks for the affirmation," Spencer grinned.

"Give her a hug for me."

"Will do."

CHAPTER SEVENTEEN

C oroner Timothy Eckels had helped to solve yet another homicide with his findings. He'd suspected Ricin from the beginning, but couldn't be certain, never having seen its effects in person. The lab confirmed his suspicions, and with the other evidence that Detective Beckett had collected, the identification of the poison had been enough to arrest a murderer. It had been a good day.

Tim drove home lost in his own thoughts, forgetting entirely about the young woman beside him until she spoke.

"I'm so tired," Fiona yawned. "Have you ever noticed that once a case is solved that there's this like big letdown? Like an exhale?"

"No."

"You're really smart," she observed. "I've learned a ton just by watching you and listening to you. You're good at what you do." For the first time since she'd met the enigmatic mortician, she was serious and subdued.

Tim slowly turned his head, looked at her for a few seconds, then swung his eyes back to the road.

"Why do you push people away all the time? You're smart, you're hilarious, and I know that you're capable of conversation if someone is willing to try hard enough. There's gotta be a story there. Who burned you so badly that you still haven't recovered, Timmy?"

"Don't call me that," was the quiet reply.

"I'm gonna make you talk to me someday," Fiona vowed, not put off in the least by his reticence.

"Doubtful."

She smiled a tired smile and gave up for the moment, leaning her head back against the seat. They were only a couple of turns away from their respective homes, and arrived soon after. Fiona sat straight up in her seat when he pulled into her driveway to drop her off.

"Tim, look! Right there!" she whispered, pointing and grabbing his arm. "Doesn't it look like there's someone in the bushes behind your house?"

Tim squinted through his thick glasses, leaning forward and craning his neck. "No."

"I'm going to prove it to you," she growled, flinging open the door and launching herself toward his back yard.

She made a beeline toward the bushes that separated his yard from the one behind it, and found…exactly nothing. No human, no animal, nothing. She bent over, recovering from her adrenalin-fueled sprint, hands on her knees as she tried to regulate her breathing. Tim meandered over to where she was standing, a troubled look on his face.

"You probably think I'm a complete idiot now," she shook her head, still panting.

"No, actually I think I saw someone running away from the bushes before you got to them," he said quietly, scanning the area beyond his yard.

"On the one hand, that sucks, but on the other…it's awfully nice to be able to say I told you so," she managed to tease, despite sucking wind.

"It could've been nothing."

"But it could've been something," Fiona pointed out.

"It could. Would you like me to escort you to your door?"

Suppressing a smile of delight at his old-fashioned chivalry, she nodded.

"Yes, I would."

They started off toward Fiona's house and Tim stopped suddenly, the hairs on the back of his neck standing up.

"What's wrong?" Fiona asked, noting the strange look on his face.

"You've got me jumping at shadows," he shook his head and continued, occasionally glancing behind them.

"Thanks for being my bodyguard," she teased as Tim stood at the bottom step of the porch, waiting for her to unlock her door.

"I was merely being courteous."

"Uh-huh, well thanks for that, too," she replied, opening the door.

She took one step inside, and came running out again.

"Tim!" she called out, eyes wide. He'd been just about to get in the car, but closed the door and started toward the house instead. "Come up here," she ordered, waving to beckon him.

"I can't go in there," she said, one hand to her chest, leaning against the house.

"Why?"

"There's a..." she shook her head and shuddered. "Just go get it please. Make it go away."

"What is it?" Tim asked.

"Just get rid of it," she shrieked.

"Fine."

He walked over and opened the door, stepping over the threshold into the house. He stopped short when he saw what had Fiona so upset, and the color drained from his face. On Fiona's couch, as though he had every right to be there, was a huge grey tabby with golden eyes and one white paw, which he was currently licking. The cat spotted Tim and stopped in mid-lick. Slowly lowering it's paw, it mewed plaintively, watching Tim for a reaction. Tim couldn't move, couldn't speak. He heard Fiona's voice behind him.

"This is so freaky. Cats scare me. I don't know how he got in here. It's not like I left a door or window open or anything," she babbled, still frightened.

"He's my cat," Tim whispered hoarsely.

"Wait, what? I didn't know you had a cat. How come I've never seen him before?"

"Because he went missing…in Key West, before I ever moved here," he said in a monotone, clearly in shock.

"Are you trying to tell me that this cat followed you here from Key West?" Fiona was skeptical. "When did you lose him down there?"

"More than two years ago," Tim ran a shaky hand across his brow, and the cat hopped down from the sofa and began twining his way through the mortician's ankles, purring.

"That can't be him," Fiona shook her head, backing away.

"It is."

"He found you?"

"Someone did."

CHAPTER EIGHTEEN

Missy snuggled into Chas's powerful chest as they stood in front of their new home.

"I can't believe it's almost done," Missy wondered, gazing at the beautiful structure.

"Hard to believe that we'll be leaving the inn in a week and moving in here. It'll be bittersweet," Chas kissed the top of her head.

"Mmhmm...but it'll be good for us. I can focus on Cupcakes in Paradise and you can grow your new business."

"Exactly. I'm glad Spence agreed to take the caretaker's cottage. It'll be nice having him close."

"Yes, it will. He's just like the son we never had," Missy smiled fondly.

"There's another reason that I'm glad he'll be around," Chas sighed and turned toward his wife. "There's something I need to tell you."

"Okay. What is it, honey? Are you okay?"

"Yes, I'm fine. I had Spencer look into the history of this house and some bad things happened here. I don't want to go into any details, but there were some very bad people who hung out here, once upon a time. We're doing everything we can to keep track of those people, because we don't want them coming back…ever."

Missy remembered the man that she and Echo encountered and shuddered. "Is it safe here?"

Chas brushed her cheek with the back of his hand. "Between me, and Spencer, and your faithful furry friends, we'll be just fine. I just wanted you to know."

"Okay. I always feel safe with you," she stood up on her tiptoes and kissed her handsome husband's cheek."

"Oh, and the landscapers found a poisonous snake in the grass," he commented.

"What??? Maybe we don't need to move…" Missy glanced at the ground around her sandaled feet and bit her lip.

AN IMPORTANT NOTE FROM THE AUTHOR:

Dear INNcredibly Sweet readers,

It seems that we've come to the end of an era. While the adventures of Missy, Chas and the gang will continue, this book is the last in the INNcredibly Sweet Series. Since Missy and Chas will no longer own the inn in the next book, the new series will be entitled The Cupcakes in Paradise Series. All of your favorite characters, along with some new faces and personalities will be there, and will be tackling crime in the sleepy town of Calgon. Thank you for reading the INNcredibly Sweet Series – I hope you will enjoy Cupcakes in Paradise just as much, if not more, as the lives of our Calgon friends continue to evolve and grow. Writing about Missy, Chas and the others has changed my life – these characters touch my heart, and I truly hope that they do the same for you. Again, my heartfelt thanks to you all (or y'all, as Missy would say).

Hugs and Sunshine,

Summer